The HAUNTED LIBRARY

FOR RUTH

I COULDN'T HAVE ASKED FOR
A BETTER MOTHER-IN-LAW.

WITH SPECIAL THANKS TO
DAVE LARSON FOR ANSWERING
ALL MY FIRE STATION QUESTIONS
—DHB

* * * * * * * * * *

GROSSET & DUNLAP
Penguin Young Readers Group
An Imprint of Penguin Random House LLC

Text copyright © 2015 by Dori Hillestad Butler. Illustrations copyright © 2015 by Aurore Damant. All rights reserved. Published by Grosset & Dunlap, an imprint of Penguin Random House LLC, 345 Hudson Street, New York, New York 10014. GROSSET & DUNLAP is a trademark of Penguin Random House LLC. Printed in the USA.

Library of Congress Cataloging-in-Publication Data is available.

ISBN 978-0-448-48334-4 (pbk)   10 9 8 7 6 5 4 3 2 1
ISBN 978-0-448-48335-1 (hc)   10 9 8 7 6 5 4 3 2 1

The HAUNTED LIBRARY

THE GHOST AT THE FIRE STATION

BY DORI HILLESTAD BUTLER
ILLUSTRATED BY AURORE DAMANT

GROSSET & DUNLAP * AN IMPRINT OF PENGUIN RANDOM HOUSE

GHOSTLY GLOSSARY

EXPAND
When ghosts make themselves larger

GLOW
What ghosts do so humans can see them

HAUNT
Where ghosts live

PASS THROUGH
When ghosts travel through walls, doors, and other solid objects

SHRINK
When ghosts make themselves smaller

SKIZZY
When ghosts feel sick to their stomachs

SOLIDS
What ghosts call humans

SPEW
Ghostly vomit

SWIM
When ghosts move freely through the air

TRANSFORMATION
When a ghost takes a solid object and turns it into a ghostly object

WAIL
What ghosts do so humans can hear them

CHAPTER 1

MEETING CLAIRE'S DAD

laire's phone buzzed during dinner, interrupting a big conversation her parents were having. Kaz, Little John, Beckett, and Cosmo hovered around the dining-room table.

"No, Claire," her mom said as Claire reached for her phone. "You know the rule. No phones at the dinner table."

"But it could be a case," Claire said.

"It can wait," Claire's mom said. "Your dad and I don't take cases during dinner.

You don't need to, either." She held out her hand. Claire's parents ran a detective agency out of their home above the library, and held a strict "no work during dinner" policy.

Claire groaned and gave the phone to her mother.

"You'll get it back after dinner," her mom promised. She laid the phone in her lap, then turned to Claire's dad. "Now, where were we?"

"You were telling me that you used to see ghosts when you were a kid?" he said. "Real, live ghosts." Kaz could tell he didn't quite believe it.

"Oh, yes. That's right." Claire's mom twirled spaghetti noodles around her fork. "I started seeing them when I was around nine. Like Claire."

"And you saw ghosts when you were

that age, too?" Claire's dad asked Grandma Karen. Grandma Karen was Claire's mom's mother.

"Yes," Grandma Karen replied. "I don't remember if I was eight or nine. Somewhere in there." She took another bite of pasta.

"But neither of you sees ghosts now." Claire's dad's eyes shifted back and forth between the two women.

"No," they said at the same time.

"Not unless they're glowing," Grandma Karen added. "That's what ghosts do when they want us to see them."

"I can see ghosts when they're not glowing!" Claire piped in. "I'm the only one in the family who can."

No one knew why Claire could see and hear ghosts when they weren't glowing or wailing. It was a mystery!

And no one knew why Claire's mom
and grandma couldn't see or hear ghosts
anymore. Kaz hated to think that one day
Claire might not be able to see or hear
him. It made him want to work harder on
his glowing and wailing skills.

"There are three ghosts in this room
with us right now," Claire added. "Four, if
you count the ghost dog."

"Woof! Woof!" Cosmo barked as he
swam in a circle around Claire's dad.

"I don't know why all the solids who live here need to know about us," Beckett grumbled.

"Don't call us solids!" Claire narrowed her eyes at Beckett.

Claire's dad looked right through Beckett. "Who are you talking to?" he asked Claire.

"Beckett," Claire replied, her mouth full of spaghetti. "He's one of the ghosts here. I don't like it when he calls us solids. That's why he does it."

"Hmph," Beckett grunted.

Claire swallowed her food. "The other ghosts are Kaz and Little John. Kaz is my age. Little John is his six-year-old brother."

"Maybe . . . it . . . would . . . help . . . if . . . he . . . could . . . see . . . us," Little John wailed as a bluish glow filled his body. "See, . . . Claire's . . . dad? . . . Here . . . I . . . am! . . . Over . . . here!" He waved his arms.

Claire's dad's mouth fell open.

"Dad, meet Little John." Claire nodded toward Kaz's little brother.

Claire's dad blinked, then rubbed his eyes and looked again at Little John.

Kaz wished he could glow and wail so Claire's dad could meet him, too. But he couldn't.

There was something else he could

do to show Claire's dad he was here, though. He dove down to the table and picked up the salt shaker.

Claire's dad's eyes opened wider. Since he couldn't see Kaz, it looked like the salt shaker was floating in midair.

Kaz had just learned how to pick up solid objects, so he couldn't hang on to the salt shaker for long. He held it carefully between the tip of his thumb and second finger, then transformed it into a ghostly salt shaker. It floated in the air beside Kaz's hand, but Claire's dad couldn't see it anymore.

"Where did the salt shaker go?" Claire's dad asked.

"It's still there," Claire said. "You can't see it because Kaz transformed it."

"Kaz can't glow or wail like other ghosts," Claire's mom explained. "But

he can transform things. That means he can turn solid objects into ghostly objects, and he can turn ghostly objects into solid objects. It's a very rare skill."

Kaz felt proud when he heard Claire's mom say that.

Claire's dad rubbed the back of his neck. "So where did all these ghosts come from?" he asked. "Why are they here?"

"I don't know where Beckett came from," Claire said. "But Kaz and Little John used to live in an old schoolhouse with the rest of their family. Then one day last summer, some people tore down the schoolhouse, and Kaz and his family ended up outside. The wind blew Kaz here. For a long time he didn't know what happened to anyone else in his family. But we found Cosmo when we were out solving a case. And you know that purple house on Marion Street? That's where the wind blew Little John. The other ghosts who lived there told him there were ghosts in the library, so he came here inside a library book and found Kaz. We don't know where the rest of their family is."

"We . . . know . . . where . . . our . . . grandma . . . and . . . grandpop . . . are . . . ," Little John wailed.

"Oh, yeah," Claire said. "We found their grandma and grandpa at the nursing home."

Claire's dad jumped when Little John's glow went out. "Now where'd that ghost go?" he asked.

"He's still there," Claire said. "He just ran out of energy. It takes a lot of energy for ghosts to glow brightly enough and wail loudly enough so we can see and hear them."

Claire's dad rubbed the back of his neck some more.

"I know it's a lot to think about." Claire's mom patted her husband's arm. "But I've been wanting to share our little family secret with you for a while."

Claire's phone buzzed again in her mom's lap. Her mom glared.

"What?" Claire said, throwing her hands into the air. "I can't help it if someone is calling me. They don't know we're having dinner."

The look on Claire's mom's face softened. "That's true," she said as Claire's phone continued to buzz. She turned back to Claire's dad. "Do you have any questions?"

"Yes. Am I ever going to see the salt shaker again?" Claire's dad asked.

"Oh!" Kaz said. "Here you go."

He transformed the salt shaker and it "reappeared" in midair, then fell to the table with a thump.

Claire's dad picked it up and turned it around. Kaz had a feeling it wasn't just the disappearing and reappearing salt shaker that Claire's dad had to think about. It was everything Claire and her mom and her grandma had just told him. Plus seeing Little John with his own eyes.

"Don't worry, Dad. You'll get used to the ghosts," Claire said.

After dinner, Claire's mom returned her cell phone as promised.

"I've got voice mail!" Claire said as she skipped up the stairs to her bedroom. Kaz and Little John swam beside her and listened while Claire played the message back:

"Hi, Claire? This is Brynlee Larson. We don't really know each other because we're not in the same class. But we're in the same grade. And I think you're in my brother's class. Do you know RJ Larson? He's here, too."

Another voice said, *"Hi."*

Brynlee continued: *"Anyway, we're calling because we heard you solve ghost mysteries. Is that true? If it is, call us back. Or talk to one of us at school tomorrow. We've got a . . . situation we want to talk to you about. Okay, bye."*

"Hmm," Claire said. "Sounds like we may have a new case! I'll call her back right now."

CHAPTER 2

A VISIT TO THE FIRE STATION

laire's cat, Thor, growled at Kaz and Little John as he strolled beneath them. Claire was still talking with Brynlee on the phone.

"Why doesn't Claire's cat like us?" Little John asked. "We never did anything to it."

"Well, Cosmo chases him," Kaz pointed out.

"Cosmo isn't here. He's downstairs with Claire's grandma," Little John said.

Kaz shrugged. "Some solid animals just don't like ghosts very much."

"Funny you should mention that, Kaz," Claire said as she tossed her phone onto her bed. "Brynlee and RJ have a new dog named Sparky. Well, Sparky really belongs to their dad. He's a firefighter, so they got Sparky to be a fire station mascot. Anyway, everything was fine at first. But now there's this room at the fire station that Sparky won't go in. He just stands in the doorway and barks at something in there. No one knows what he's barking at."

"Is he barking at a ghost?" Little John asked.

"That's what Brynlee and RJ think," Claire replied. "There have been some strange things happening at the fire station, too. Some of the firefighters have heard weird noises during the night. One of them even saw a ghost. That's why Brynlee and RJ want me to come over. They want me to catch the ghost."

"I wonder if the ghost is Mom or Pops or Finn," Little John said.

Finn was Kaz and Little John's big brother. He got lost in the Outside even before the old schoolhouse was torn down. No one in the family knew where he was now.

"Where's your water bottle, Claire?" Little John rubbed his hands together. The rubbing made his hands glow.

"Not so fast, Little John," Claire said. "We aren't going now. It's almost bedtime. We'll go tomorrow after school."

"Aw," Little John groaned.

"I'm not sure Little John and I should go then, either," Kaz said.

"Why not?" Claire asked.

"Yeah. Why not?" Little John asked. The glow faded from his hands.

"Because that dog probably doesn't like ghosts," Kaz said. "That's why he barks, right? Who knows what he'll do if two more ghosts show up?"

"Yes, but lots of ghosts don't trust people like me," Claire said. "Sparky might not be happy to see you, but I bet the ghost at the fire station would be *very* happy to see you."

"Claire's right," Little John said. "Mom or Pops might swim away from her. But they wouldn't swim away from us."

Kaz had to admit that Claire and Little John had a point. "Okay. We'll go," he said finally.

"Tomorrow," Claire said again. "After school."

✳ ✳ ✳ ✳ ✳ ✳ ✳ ✳ ✳ ✳ ✳ ✳ ✳ ✳ ✳ ✳ ✳

Kaz had seen both Brynlee and RJ at Claire's school before, but he'd never seen them *together* until they stepped out onto their front porch.

"Those two solids have the same hair and the same face," Little John said as he and Kaz hovered inside Claire's water

bottle. Beckett and Cosmo were back at the library.

"They're twins," Kaz said.

"It's cool that you live so close to the fire station," Claire said to the twins. "Isn't it right around the corner?"

"There's a shortcut through our backyard," Brynlee and RJ said at the same time. They looked at each other and slapped high fives.

"We keep saying the exact same thing—" Brynlee began.

"—at the exact same time," RJ finished.

"It's a twin thing," Brynlee said.

"Cool," Claire said again.

"Come on," RJ said, hopping down the porch stairs. "We'll show you the shortcut." They led Claire around the house and through the bushes at the back of the yard.

"This is the back of the fire station." Brynlee pointed at the tall brick building. "We can go in that door over there." She ran ahead and opened the door.

"Wow!" Kaz said, wide-eyed, as Claire stepped inside the fire station garage. Neither he nor Little John had ever been this close to real fire trucks before. The trucks were so big. So red. So shiny.

As soon as the door was closed, the ghosts passed through the side of Claire's water bottle and expanded to full size.

"What are all these trucks?" Little John asked as he swam alongside a truck with a long ladder stretched across the top.

"Do they have special names?" Kaz floated above another truck and gazed down at all the strange dials.

"Do the fire trucks have special names?" Claire asked Brynlee and RJ.

"Well, this is the chief's car, and this is just an ATV," RJ said as he touched another truck. It was much smaller than the ones Kaz and Little John were looking at.

"What's an ATV?" Claire asked.

"It's a truck that can go off road," RJ said. He pointed at the truck by Kaz. "That one over there is a pumper truck, and the one next to it is a ladder truck. That ladder can reach the top of any building in Kirksville."

"Wow," Claire said.

"Come on," Brynlee said. "Sparky's probably inside with Dad."

Kaz and Little John had to swim fast to catch up to Claire, Brynlee, and RJ, who were tromping up the stairs at the back of the garage. Brynlee opened a door at the top of the stairs, and they all stepped into a long white hallway. There was a little room off to the left where a woman in a uniform sat in front of three computer screens. She had her back to the kids. A large window in front of her looked out over the inside of the garage.

"That's the radio room," RJ said to Claire. "The lady in there answers nine-one-one calls and sounds the alarm when there's a fire."

They continued down the hall to a large open room with lots of desks. There was a counter at the far end of the room. All the people in there were wearing uniforms and looked very busy.

On the other side of the counter was the main door to the fire station.

"Hello, kids." One of the firefighters waved from his desk. A large white dog with black spots was curled up on a red pillow beside him. The dog raised his head when the kids walked in.

"Hi, Dad," Brynlee said. "This is our new friend, Claire. Claire, this is our dad."

"Welcome, Claire! I'm Dick." The

firefighter stood up and shook Claire's hand. "And this is Sparky." He gave the dog a pat on the head. "You better say hello to him, too."

Claire tried to pet Sparky, but Sparky got up and trotted over to the ghosts. He sniffed Little John's foot. Then he turned to Kaz's foot.

"Ahh!" Kaz cried out. He shot up to the ceiling and stayed there.

"Woof! Woof!" Sparky barked cheerfully and leaped at Kaz. He wagged his tail and danced around on his hind legs.

Dick laughed. "Sparky likes you, Claire," he said. "He's showing off for you."

Little John snorted. "He's not showing off for Claire. He's trying to get Kaz to come down here so he can sniff him."

"I don't want him to sniff me," Kaz said.

"Why not?" Little John asked. "He's not going to hurt us." He drifted down to Sparky's level and called, "Here, Sparky!"

Sparky turned and charged right through Little John.

Little John giggled.

Sparky looked up at Kaz. "Woof! Woof!" he barked again, his tail wagging.

"He must *really* like you, Claire," RJ said. "He doesn't normally run back and forth like that."

"That's great," Claire said uneasily. Sparky was obviously much more interested in Kaz and Little John than he was in Claire. But no one else could see that.

"Don't be such a scaredy ghost, Kaz," Little John said. "Come down here so Sparky can sniff you."

Kaz slowly drifted down. As soon as he was low enough, Sparky dashed through

him. It made Kaz feel a little bit skizzy.

"I think Sparky likes ghosts," Little John said.

"Well, he likes *us,* anyway," Kaz said. It didn't sound as though he liked the other ghost at the fire station.

"So, where's the room that Sparky doesn't like to go in?" Claire asked the twins.

"We'll show you," they said at the same time.

"Come on, Sparky." Brynlee patted her leg, and Sparky trotted after her. She led everyone down the hallway, past a kitchen, past two rooms with small beds, all the way to the room at the end of the hall.

Sparky stopped at the doorway, sat down, and began to howl. "Aroooooooooooooo!"

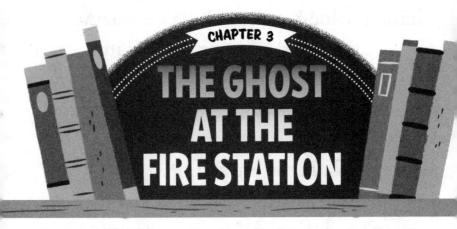

CHAPTER 3

THE GHOST AT THE FIRE STATION

parky lunged toward the room, but refused to step through the doorway. "Arooooooooooo!" he howled again.

"See what I mean? He won't come in here no matter what you do," Brynlee said. She hopped over Sparky to get into the room. Claire and RJ did the same.

"Ar-ar-arooooooooooo!" Sparky howled.

Little John put his hands to his ears. "He's loud!"

Kaz agreed. He and Little John
swam over Sparky and into the room.
It looked like some sort of family room
or activity room. There was a large TV
on the wall in front of them. A couch
and two chairs. A table with a green top
and a bunch of balls on it. But if there
were any other ghosts in here, they were
hiding.

"Mom? Pops? Finn?" Kaz called as he
turned all around.

"Come out, come out, wherever you
are!" Little John added.

No ghosts came out.

The twins tried to get the dog to
come into the room with them. "Sparky,
come! Come here, boy!" They sounded
happy and excited.

"Woof! Woof!" Sparky barked as
he raised his rear end in the air, put his

paws down, and hopped around. He refused to enter the room.

RJ pulled a dog treat out of his pocket and held it out to Sparky. "Here, boy! Come get the treat!"

Sparky still wouldn't come.

"He has come in here before, right?" Claire said.

"Yes. All the time," Brynlee said.

"But he doesn't come in anymore," RJ said. He turned to Claire. "Didn't you say you have some sort of equipment for finding ghosts?"

"Oh, yeah," Claire said. She opened her bag and pulled out her ghost glass and her ghost catcher.

"WOOF! WOOF!" Sparky barked. "Aroooooooooooooo!"

Claire put her ghost glass to her eye and wandered around the room.

When she came to a row of cabinets, she glanced at Kaz and Little John.

"You think the ghost might be hiding in there?" Kaz asked.

She nodded slightly.

"You check these cabinets," Little John told Kaz. "I'll check the ones over there." He swam across the room and through another cabinet door.

Kaz took a deep breath. It was a good thing he could pass through solid objects now. He stepped into the door. First a foot, then his leg, then the rest of his body. He only felt a *little* skizzy this time.

He rolled to his back. It was dark inside this cabinet. And even though he was fully inside the cabinet, it still felt like he was passing through something. Something heavy.

Oh. Blankets. The cabinet was full of blankets.

Kaz passed through the wall from one cabinet and into the next one. There were books in that one. And board games in the last one.

No ghosts.

Kaz returned to the TV room. Claire looked at him expectantly. He shook his head.

"No ghosts in these cabinets, either," Little John said. "I don't think Mom, Pops, or Finn is here. They'd come out if they heard our voices."

Kaz agreed. So who was the ghost at

the fire station? And where was he or she hiding?

"WOOF! WOOF! WOOF!" Sparky barked and danced around in the doorway.

Claire turned to Brynlee and RJ. "This is very strange, but I'm not detecting any ghosts in this room," she said.

RJ scowled. "Does that stuff really work?" he asked. "Look at Sparky! There's obviously a ghost in here."

There were *two* ghosts in here: Kaz and Little John. But Brynlee and RJ didn't know that. And Sparky didn't seem to mind being in the same room with them.

"Of course it works," Claire said. "Are there any other rooms here that Sparky won't go into?"

"No," the twins said at the same time.

"Can we take him into all the other rooms to be sure?" Claire asked.

"If you want," RJ said with a shrug. "Come on, Sparky."

The dog trotted happily after the solid kids. He glanced up at Kaz and Little John and let out a friendly *woof*, his tail swishing from side to side.

Sparky walked right into the two bedrooms, the kitchen, the bathrooms, and the office area without any problem. But when they returned to the TV room, he dropped to his belly and refused to go inside.

"Have you guys ever actually *seen* a ghost here?" Claire asked.

The twins glanced at each other. "No," they said together.

"A couple of the firefighters have, though," RJ said.

"Can I talk to them?" Claire asked. She put her ghost-hunting equipment

back in her bag and pulled out her notebook.

"Sure," Brynlee said, leading everyone back down the hall.

"Hey, Dad?" RJ said when they got to the office. "Where's Tom?"

Dick looked up. "He and Janelle went out to the garage."

"Yay! We get to see the fire trucks again." Little John rubbed his hands together as they wafted down the hall.

Sparky let out a short *woof* when he saw Little John's hands glowing.

Kaz grabbed Little John's hands. "Don't do that," he said. "Do you want everyone to see your hands glowing?"

"I can't help it. I'm excited," Little John said.

RJ pushed open the door to the garage, and Kaz got a quick peek inside as Claire,

Sparky, and the twins hurried past him.

"Oh no," Kaz said, backing away from the garage. He grabbed his brother, and the door closed in front of them.

"Why did you do that?" Little John asked.

"The back door is open," Kaz said.

Little John groaned. An open door meant the ghosts could be sucked into the Outside and blown away.

"But it's a big garage," Little John said. "And that back door is a small door. We'll just stay away from it. Like we do at the library."

"Well . . . ," Kaz said. He could tell Little John really wanted to see the fire trucks again. "Okay. Just promise me you'll stay *far* away from the open door."

"I will," Little John said. The ghosts passed through the closed door and

glided along the ceiling of the fire station garage.

"Woof! Woof!" Sparky ran below the ghosts.

"Check out the inside of this fire truck!" Little John said. He darted through the driver's side window and into the cab of the ladder truck.

But Kaz was more interested in what the firefighters had to say.

"What do you want to know about our ghost?" a man with glasses asked Claire. His name badge said TOM.

Claire opened her notebook and got ready to write. "Everything!" she said. "What does it look like? How many times have you seen it? What does it do?"

"Well, I've never gotten a real good look at it," Tom said. "I've just seen

a shadowy figure wandering around during the night."

"Man or woman?" Claire asked.

"I'm not really sure," Tom said.

"Definitely a man," a lady firefighter said as she came around from the other side of the fire truck. She had a big hose in her hand, and her name badge read JANELLE. "An *old* man, it sounds like, by the way he moans and groans."

"I've never heard any moaning or groaning," a heavyset, dark-haired firefighter said. His name badge said DAVID.

"Really?" Janelle raised an eyebrow. "The ghost has never woken you up?"

"It's woken *me* up," Tom said.

"The moaning and groaning hasn't woken me up," David said. "But I'll tell you what did wake me up last night.

Someone or some*thing* pulled the covers off me!"

Janelle nodded. "That happened to me two nights ago. In fact, I found my blanket way out in the hallway! Our ghost steals blankets. Write that down," she told Claire.

Claire did. Then she asked Janelle, "Did you see the ghost?"

"Not well enough to describe," Janelle replied. "Like Tom said, it's a shadowy figure."

"Where did you see him? In that TV room?" Claire asked.

"Yes, there. And in the hallway and the kitchen—" Janelle started to say, but she was cut off by a loud alarm that rang out through the garage.

"FIRE!"

CHAPTER 4

FIRE!

parky's howls were loud, but the alarm was even louder! Kaz pressed his hands to his ears. It didn't help.

Firefighters rushed to the garage. Some burst through the door at the top of the stairs. Others slid down the pole. They hopped into boots, grabbed coats and helmets from the hooks, and ran to the trucks.

The big garage doors started to rise. Kaz didn't want to be sucked into the

Outside. He swam back . . . back . . . back as hard as he could. But not too far back, because the back door was open, too! He swam up to the glass window where the lady sat in front of all those computer screens. The radio room, RJ called it. Kaz sailed through the window and into the room.

Safe.

"Little John?" Kaz said as he turned around. Where was Little John? Was he still inside the ladder truck?

Kaz wafted back over to the window and looked down into the garage. He didn't see Little John anywhere.

The radio-room lady had something on her head that attached to a small microphone in front of her mouth. "You're heading to 1024 Elm Street," she said into the microphone.

One by one, with lights flashing and sirens blaring, the trucks pulled out of the garage below and drove away.

And before anyone knew what was happening, Sparky charged after them! Right into the street.

Kaz couldn't hear Brynlee and RJ over the sound of the alarm, but he saw them say something to each other as they waved their arms in the air. Then they hurried after Sparky.

Claire glanced up at Kaz. She said something to him, but Kaz couldn't make it out.

"What . . . ?" Kaz wailed as Claire set her bag and water bottle on a bench. "What . . . did . . . you . . . say, . . . Claire?"

"Who said that?" the radio lady asked, looking all around.

Claire grabbed a rope from a hook above the bench and ran after the twins. Leaving Kaz behind.

"CLAIRE . . . ," Kaz wailed again. Louder this time.

All of a sudden, he felt tired. Really tired. Like he had no energy.

"Who's Claire?" the radio lady asked, looking right at him.

Kaz blinked. Was the radio lady talking to him? Could she see him?

"What? Am I glowing?" he asked. Was that why he was suddenly so tired? He looked down at himself. No, he wasn't glowing. The radio lady couldn't see him. But she had definitely *heard* him say Claire's name.

"I was wailing, wasn't I?" he cried in amazement. "You heard me wailing!"

But the radio lady didn't hear that because Kaz wasn't wailing anymore.

The alarm stopped. The big garage doors rumbled as they started to close. With a shrug, the lady turned her attention back to the screens in front of her.

"Engine one is in service," came a voice from a speaker in front of her.

How did I do it? Kaz wondered. He didn't know, because he hadn't been trying to wail. The wail had just come out. But that was how it happened with most of his ghost skills. The first time he got a skill right, he did it without even thinking about it.

Maybe wailing had something to do with how LOUD a ghost said something. It probably had something to do with stomach muscles, too, Kaz thought, because his stomach muscles ached.

He tried tightening his stomach muscles. Tight! Tight! Tight! As tight as he could make them. Then he wailed, "Wooooooo . . ."

The radio lady moved the microphone away from her mouth. "Who said that? Who's there?" she asked, looking all around.

It worked!

"I-it's . . . me . . . ," Kaz wailed.
"Kaz . . ." His stomach muscles gave out.
He couldn't wail anymore.

"Kaz? Kaz who?" the radio lady asked.
"Are you the fire station ghost?"

"No, I'm just Kaz. I'm a different ghost,"
he said. It came out as words, not wails,
so the lady couldn't hear him. And Kaz
didn't have the energy to try wailing
again.

"Ladder one is arriving on the scene,"
came a voice through the speaker.

"Engine one is two minutes out,"
came another voice.

"Well, whoever you are, I can't talk
to you right now," the lady said. "I'm
working." She scooted closer to the
microphone and turned her attention to
the screens in front of her.

Kaz didn't want to bother the lady. Or keep her from important work. But he wanted to know what was happening. Was Sparky okay? Would Claire, Brynlee, and RJ come back soon? And where was Little John?

Kaz passed through the glass window and into the garage. While the big doors at the front of the garage were down, the back door still stood wide open. Kaz stayed far away from that door.

"Little John?" he called as he swam along the ceiling. "Are you still here?"

No response.

Kaz didn't really expect a response. He didn't think Little John was in the fire station. He hoped his little brother was still safe inside the ladder truck. Maybe that was why Sparky ran after the fire truck? Because he knew Little John was inside?

Or . . . maybe Sparky saw Little John blow into the Outside.

Kaz drifted down along one of the big garage doors and peered through the small windows at the top of the door. He didn't see Little John drifting around in the Outside. He didn't see Claire, Brynlee, RJ, or Sparky, either.

Kaz sighed as he swam away from the garage door. How long would it be before anyone came back?

He swam back up to the glass window and passed through into the radio room again.

"No sign of smoke or fire yet," came a voice from the speaker.

Then he swam out into the hallway and all through the rest of the fire station. The radio lady was the only solid person in the whole building.

Kaz wafted through the room with all the desks and over to a window. Now he could see Claire, Brynlee, and RJ running back toward the station.

Hooray! Sparky was with them! He had a rope tied to his collar. Brynlee held the other end of the rope as they ran.

Kaz backstroked away from the door just in time before Brynlee shoved

it open. Sparky charged in ahead of everyone.

"Don't ever run away like that again, Sparky," Brynlee scolded.

With his tail wagging, Sparky ran right to Kaz. Kaz gritted his teeth as Sparky passed through him, then turned around and passed through him again.

"Woof! Woof!" Sparky barked, like this was a fun game. Then he ran around the whole station, sniffing . . . sniffing . . . sniffing like he was looking for something.

"What's he looking for?" Brynlee asked.

"Maybe his ball?" RJ said. He crawled under a desk, pulled out a green ball, and tossed it to Sparky. "Here, boy. Is this what you're looking for?"

Sparky ignored the ball and ran back to Kaz. "Woof! Woof!"

Kaz had a feeling Sparky was looking for Little John.

"I don't know where he is," Kaz told the dog. "I was hoping you knew."

Just then, they all heard a garage door going up.

"The fire trucks are back," Brynlee said.

"Already?" Claire said.

"It was probably a false alarm," RJ said. "Most fire calls are."

Kaz wondered if Little John was back, too. He swam into the radio room and watched the trucks pull into the garage. As soon as the garage doors were down, he passed through the glass window and paddled over to the ladder truck. He peered through the windshield.

Little John was not inside.

CHAPTER 5

THE BIG SEARCH

Kaz swam back through the fire station. "We have to go!" he told Claire. "Little John is missing. We have to find him!"

Claire nodded slightly to Kaz, then turned to Brynlee and RJ. "I'm sorry we didn't find your ghost today. I'll come back tomorrow and search some more."

"Let's . . . go . . . ," Kaz wailed.

Brynlee gasped. RJ's mouth fell open. Claire had a funny look on her face. She was the only one who could actually see

Kaz. But everyone else had just *heard* him.

"That was the ghost!" the twins said at the same time.

Uh-oh. Kaz hadn't meant to wail. Once again, it had just come out.

"Do you see it?" Brynlee grabbed Claire's arm.

"No," Claire lied as she looked straight at Kaz.

"Get out your ghost-hunting equipment," RJ said. "The ghost is here. We all heard it."

"No, Claire," Kaz cried in his normal voice. "We don't have time for that. We have to look for Little John. Where's your water bottle?" It was usually on her shoulder. Or in her hand. But Kaz didn't see it.

"My stuff is out in the garage," Claire said. "But . . . I don't know what you're talking about, RJ. I don't know what you guys heard that makes you think there's a ghost in here. I didn't hear anything. And look at Sparky. I don't think he heard anything, either."

Sparky was curled up on the red pillow next to Brynlee and RJ's dad's desk. Chasing fire trucks was exhausting.

"Huh," Brynlee said. "She's right.

Sparky isn't upset. Maybe we just thought we heard something."

"But we both heard it. Even if Claire didn't," RJ said.

Brynlee shrugged. "Must have been another one of those weird twin things. We imagined the same thing."

"I really have to go," Claire said.

The twins led Claire down the hall and out to the garage. Kaz followed close behind.

There were a lot of firefighters bustling around in the garage, cleaning equipment, winding hoses, and shining the trucks.

Claire grabbed her bag and water bottle from the bench where she'd left them. Kaz shrank down . . . down . . . down . . . and passed through the side of the water bottle.

"Come back and see us again." David

waved as Claire opened a small door at the front of the garage.

Once they were safely outside, Claire said to Kaz, "You wailed in there! You figured out how to wail."

"Sort of," Kaz said. "But I don't want to talk about that. We have to find Little John!"

"I don't know where he could be," Claire said as she started down the street. "I saw him go inside the ladder truck before the alarm sounded. But I don't know if he was still in there when the fire fighters drove away. What if he blew out when they opened the doors?"

If that was the case, they might never find Little John. The wind would have blown him away.

But they had to try.

"We should go to where the fire trucks

went," Kaz said. "Maybe we'll see him blowing around there."

Claire stopped walking. "But we don't know where they went."

"Yes, we do," Kaz said. "I heard it in the radio room. They went to 1024 Elm Street."

"Okay," Claire said. "Let's find Elm Street." She pulled out her phone to get directions and started walking again.

Along the way, Kaz turned all around inside Claire's water bottle. If Little John was out there somewhere, Kaz didn't want to miss him.

It didn't take long to reach 1024 Elm Street. There were no signs of a fire. No signs that fire trucks had even been there recently.

"Do you see Little John?" Kaz asked, squinting.

"No," Claire replied. "Do you?"

"No," Kaz said glumly.

They walked all around the building. No luck.

"Which direction is the wind coming from?" Kaz asked. "Maybe we could follow the wind to see where it might have blown him."

"We can try," Claire said, but she didn't sound hopeful. "I think it's blowing behind us."

Claire walked and walked . . . all the way to the edge of town. Kaz gazed out over an empty field. *Little John, where are you?* he wondered.

"I'm sorry, Kaz," Claire said softly. "It's almost dinnertime. We have to go home. We can look for Little John again tomorrow."

Kaz's throat felt tight. "Okay," he choked. But he had a bad feeling about this. Little John was gone. Maybe forever this time.

* * * * * * * * * * * * * * *

"I miss the little guy, too," Beckett said later that night. Claire and the ghosts had gathered in the library turret room.

Kaz hugged Cosmo and peered out the window into the darkness. Little John had to be out there somewhere. *Somewhere.*

"We shouldn't have brought him," Claire said. "We should've left him here with Beckett and Cosmo."

They should have, Kaz agreed.

"What's going on in here?" Claire's dad asked from the doorway.

Claire's mom peered over his shoulder. "You look upset, honey," she said to Claire.

"We lost Little John at the fire station," Claire said. "There was a fire call, and when the big garage doors went up, Sparky ran out. In all the excitement, we somehow lost Little John. We don't know what happened to him."

"Oh, dear," said her mom.

"That's the little brother, right?" Claire's dad asked.

Claire nodded.

Her dad stepped into the room. "I'm sorry," he said, resting a hand on Claire's back. "And tell your friend, the big brother ghost, that I'm sorry, too. Okay?"

If Kaz wasn't so upset, he'd try and wail back to Claire's dad. But he couldn't gather the energy to try right now. He just couldn't.

"He knows," Claire told her dad.

"Did you find the ghost at the fire station?" Claire's mom asked.

Claire shook her head. "We didn't find the ghost we were hired to find. *And* we lost Little John. Today was a bad day," she said glumly.

"Well, tomorrow's a new day," Claire's mom said, trying to sound hopeful. "Maybe things will look better in the morning."

Kaz didn't see how they could.

69

CHAPTER 6

A MESSAGE FOR CLAIRE

Y ou can't just mope around the library all day," Claire told Kaz as she packed her bag the next morning. "Come to school with me."

"I don't want to," Kaz said.

"We'll look for Little John after school," Claire said. "We should go over to the fire station and look for that ghost again, too."

"I said no!" Kaz snapped. The last

thing he wanted to do was search for the ghost at the fire station. That was how they'd lost Little John in the first place.

"Kaz," Beckett said, closing the book in his hand. "You should go to school with the solid. This isn't the first time you and Little John have been apart. I'm sure your brother is fine."

They didn't understand. They couldn't understand. Beckett didn't have a family. And Claire had never been separated from hers. They didn't know how it felt to lose someone, then find them, and then get separated again. It felt worse than being apart the first time.

"I know you think I don't understand," Beckett said. "But I do. I lost my family years ago."

"You have a family?" Claire said with surprise.

Beckett scowled. "Of course I have a family. Everyone has a family."

"Where are they? What happened to them?" Kaz asked.

"They blew away. Just like your family," Beckett said. "But I didn't search for them. I didn't make friends with a solid girl who wanted to form a ghost detective agency and help ghosts. I stayed here in the library and felt sorry for myself."

Claire walked over to Beckett. "It's not too late," she said softly. "You can make friends with me right now. You could even join C & K Ghost Detectives if you want."

"I don't think so," Beckett said. "Not at my age. But, Kaz, you should go with Claire." It was the first time Kaz had heard Beckett call Claire by her name.

Kaz had to admit that sitting around the library feeling sorry for himself wasn't going to accomplish anything. He and Claire still had a case to solve. He didn't want Sparky to be afraid of a room just because he'd seen a ghost in there. Kaz wanted to find that ghost and tell him to be nice to Sparky. It's what Little John would want him to do.

"Okay, I'll come to school with you, Claire. And then we can go over to the fire station after that," Kaz said. He shrank down . . . down . . . down . . . and swam into the water bottle.

"Good," Claire said, hoisting the strap from the bottle onto her shoulder. "See you later, Beckett."

* * * * * * * * * * * * * * *

When they got to school, Brynlee and RJ were waiting for Claire by her locker.

"Guess what?" Brynlee said.

"What?" Claire asked as she opened her locker. She set her water bottle on the shelf inside.

Brynlee and RJ glanced over their shoulders, then put their heads close to Claire's. "Last night our dad slept over at the fire station," Brynlee said in a low voice. "When he came home for breakfast, he said he saw the ghost during the night. It even talked to him."

"What did the ghost say?" Claire asked.

"It said, 'Tell RJ and Brynlee to bring Claire to the fire station. Tell her to come as soon as possible,'" RJ said.

Kaz passed through the side of the water bottle and swam into the middle of their circle. "Why would the ghost ask for you?" he asked Claire. "How does he or she even know your name?"

"Did your dad say anything else about the ghost?" Claire asked the twins.

"Just that it was a young boy," RJ said.

Kaz blinked. *A young boy?*

"We'll check it out after school," Claire said as she closed her locker door.

Kaz swam next to Claire's ear. "Little John is a young boy. The ghost must be Little John. That's how he knows your name," he said. "The ghost is Little John!"

Claire veered into the girls' bathroom. She motioned for Kaz to follow.

Kaz felt a little funny about that. He wasn't a girl. But Claire clearly wanted him to come, so he darted in behind her just before the door closed.

"That ghost could be Little John. But remember, there's another ghost at the fire station, too. A ghost that Sparky doesn't like for some reason. That's why we were at the fire station to begin with."

Kaz suddenly felt worried for Little John. "Do you think the other ghost is a bad ghost?" he asked. "Like the one your mom knew when she was a kid?"

Claire's mom had a ghost friend named Molly when she was Claire's age. Back then, the library was all apartments. Claire's mom, Grandma Karen, and Molly lived in one of the apartments. One day a mean ghost named Annie came. She took things that belonged to Claire's mom and to people who lived in the other apartments and made Molly transform them. She wanted people to be afraid and move out so she could have the whole house to herself. She even pushed Molly through a wall into the Outside, and Claire's mom never saw Molly again!

What if the ghost at the fire station was like Annie?

What if Little John was at the fire station with a very mean ghost, and that mean ghost pushed *him* into the Outside?

"We'll go over to the fire station after school," Claire said.

* * * * * * * * * * * * * * * *

The kids stopped at Brynlee and RJ's house to pick up Sparky. Their dad had brought Sparky home from the fire station in the morning because the dog had been barking and howling all night.

"Why was he barking and howling so much?" Kaz asked from inside Claire's water bottle. "He likes Little John. He wouldn't bark at Little John. Not in a mean way, anyway."

But Claire couldn't talk to Kaz because Brynlee and RJ were there.

"Woof! Woof!" Sparky barked cheerfully when the kids went inside the house.

"Hey, boy," RJ said, patting his head. Brynlee and Claire stopped to pet him, too.

Sparky sniffed at Claire's water bottle. "Woof! Woof!" he barked again, his tail wagging. Then he licked the outside of the bottle.

"Hi, Sparky." Kaz waved at the dog.

"Sparky must be really thirsty," Brynlee said.

"Over here, Sparky," RJ said, pointing to a full bowl of water.

But the dog wasn't thirsty. "Woof! Woof!" he barked. He licked Claire's water bottle again. He wanted to play with Kaz!

"Sparky can get water at the fire station," Brynlee said. "Let's go. I want to find out why this ghost wanted us to bring Claire as soon as possible." She snapped Sparky's leash to his collar, and they all trooped over to the fire station through the backyard. Just like they'd done the day before.

As they got close to the fire station door, Sparky pulled on the leash and started barking again. But this time it was NOT a friendly bark.

"WOOF! WOOF! WOOF!" he said. His ears and tail stood straight up.

RJ tried to pull the dog through the door, but Sparky dug his paws into the grass and refused to go inside. "Ar-ar-aroooooooooo!" he howled.

"What's the matter with him?" Brynlee asked.

Kaz was wondering the same thing. "What's the matter, Sparky?" he asked from inside Claire's water bottle.

Sparky turned to lick Claire's water bottle right. Then he howled some more. "Aroooooo!"

It wasn't just the TV room anymore. Now Sparky didn't want to go inside the fire station at all!

CHAPTER 7

GHOST HUNTING

Was the other ghost in the garage now? Was that the problem?

Kaz couldn't see the whole garage from inside Claire's water bottle, but he could see a lot of it. He didn't see any ghosts in there.

"Maybe we should take Sparky around front and see if he'll go in the main door," Claire suggested.

"That's a good idea," Brynlee said.

They all ran up the grassy hill behind

the fire station and around to the front of the building. RJ pushed open the main door, and Sparky ran through it with his tail wagging. He charged into the office and went from one desk to another, greeting all the firefighters.

"Weird," Brynlee and RJ said.

"What's weird?" Dick asked. "The fact that you two have this twin thing where you say the same thing at the same time?"

"No," Brynlee said as Kaz passed through the water bottle and expanded to full size.

"You know how Sparky won't go in the TV room?" RJ said. "He was like that with the back door just now, too. He wouldn't go into the garage. We thought maybe he didn't want to go into the fire station at all anymore. But he didn't mind coming in this door."

"That's a funny fire station mascot," David said with a laugh. "A dog who refuses to go into the fire station."

Several of the other firefighters nodded in agreement.

"Let's see if he'll go into the garage from *inside* the fire station," RJ said as he headed for the back hallway. "Come on, Sparky!"

Kaz would've preferred to look for Little John, but he followed Sparky, RJ, Brynlee, and Claire down the hall. When they reached the door to the garage, RJ pulled it open.

Sparky sat down and let out a low growl.

While RJ held the door open, Brynlee walked through and turned around at the top of the stairs. "Come here, Sparky!" she said, patting her legs.

RJ tried to nudge Sparky through the
doorway from behind, but the dog refused
to go. "Aroooooooooooo!" he howled.

Little John wafted into the hallway
behind them. "*There* you guys are!" he
said to Kaz and Claire.

"Little John!" Kaz cried. He swam to
Little John and threw his arms around his
brother. "You're here! You're safe. You're
not blowing in the wind somewhere."

Sparky leaped up and wagged his tail at Little John.

"*Now* what's that dog doing?" Brynlee asked. "Why is he so excited all of a sudden?"

"Of course I'm not blowing in the wind," Little John said. "Were you worried, Kaz? I told those firefighters last night to tell you I was here."

"Yeah, but we didn't get the message until this morning," Kaz said, finally letting Little John go. "And we didn't know for sure it was you."

"Who else would it have been? Who else would have asked for Claire?" Little John asked as he tried to pet Sparky. But Sparky swam right through his hand.

"Where were you?" Kaz asked. "Last I saw, you were inside that fire truck when the alarm sounded. But when the

fire truck came back, you were gone."

"I was still inside the fire truck," Little John said. "When the firefighters opened the doors to the truck, I was afraid I was going to get sucked into the Outside. So I shrank and hid inside the glove box. I didn't know when it was safe to come out, so I stayed there for a long, long time. When I came out, the truck was back in the garage. It was nighttime, and everyone was gone."

"Hiding in the glove box was a smart idea," Kaz said.

"I know," Little John replied.

"I'm glad we found you," Claire accidentally said out loud.

"Who are you talking to, Claire?" RJ asked.

"Is it the ghost?" Brynlee asked.

"Uh . . . yeah," Claire said quickly.

"Let me get out my equipment and I'll catch it." She unzipped her bag and pulled out her ghost glass and her ghost catcher. She aimed them both at Little John.

Kaz gasped. "No!" he cried, swimming between Claire and Little John. "You can't suck my brother into that machine!" Claire's ghost catcher was really just a handheld vacuum that she'd covered in foil. She hadn't turned it on yet, but Kaz knew it was LOUD. And strong. Much stronger and *scarier* than any outside wind.

"Relax, Kaz. We'll be safe inside Claire's water bottle," Little John said.

Oh, Kaz thought. *Of course*. After all, Claire never planned to use her ghost catcher on any real ghosts. She just needed it so other solids would *think* she'd caught a ghost.

89

Kaz and Little John shrank down . . .
down . . . down . . . and passed through
the side of Claire's water bottle. Once
they were safe inside, Claire turned on
her ghost catcher. It made a terrible noise.

Claire aimed the ghost catcher at the
wall across from the radio room as the
twins stared in amazement.

"Got it," Claire said, turning off the
machine.

Several of the firefighters heard the noise and ran toward them.

"What's going on? What are you kids doing?" Dick asked.

"Claire caught the fire station ghost," Brynlee said.

Claire raised her ghost catcher. "He's in here," she said.

"Uh . . . you should know that Kaz and I aren't the only ghosts around here," Little John said from inside Claire's water bottle.

Kaz looked curiously at Little John. He wanted to ask about the other ghost. But before he could, one of the firefighters said, "So, no more moaning and groaning in the middle of the night?"

"No more blankets being pulled off us during the night?" said another firefighter.

"And Sparky will go into the garage and the TV room now?" Dick said.

"Let's find out," Brynlee said. She went back out to the garage and held the door open. "Here, Sparky. Come here, boy."

Sparky looked at Brynlee and backed away.

RJ grabbed Sparky's collar and tried to lead him into the garage, but Sparky plopped down and refused to move.

"Maybe Sparky doesn't know the ghost is gone," Brynlee said.

"Or maybe there's another ghost," Claire said.

"There's definitely another ghost. A man," Little John said. He passed back through the water bottle and expanded to full size. Kaz did the same.

"Did you see him, Little John?" Kaz asked. "Did you talk to him?"

"I saw him. But I didn't talk to him. I was . . . too scared to talk to him," Little John admitted.

"*You* were scared?" Kaz gaped at his brother. Little John wasn't afraid of anything. Or anyone.

"He was big," Little John said. "*Really* big!" He expanded to show Kaz just how big this other ghost was.

"And he was moaning really loud and banging into things. He sounded mad. That's probably why Sparky doesn't like him."

"I tell you, there was enough banging and clattering around last night for two ghosts," Dick said.

"I think there's more than one ghost, too," Tom said. "There was *a lot* of moaning and groaning last night."

"Really?" David said. "I slept through it all."

"You're such a sound sleeper, I'm surprised you don't sleep through the alarms," Dick said.

"Maybe we should all stay overnight at the fire station this weekend," Brynlee said. "Claire, too. Then if there really is another ghost here, she can catch it!"

CHAPTER 8

SLEEPOVER AT THE FIRE STATION

A sleepover at the fire station. That sounds like fun," Claire's mom said.

"So I can go?" Claire asked.

"Yes," her mom replied.

"I hope you find the fire station ghost," her dad said. "And I'm glad you found the other ghost. The one that was lost."

"Thanks, Dad," Claire said.

Little John glowed. "I . . . wasn't . . . lost . . . ," he wailed. "I . . . always . . . knew . . . where . . . I . . . was."

"Yes, well . . ." Claire's dad smiled as though he didn't know what to say to that. Kaz had a feeling Claire's dad was still getting used to the idea that there were ghosts in the library. That ghosts really existed.

"It's too bad you didn't talk to the ghost at the fire station," Kaz said to Little John while Claire packed her bag.

Little John rubbed Cosmo's belly. "I told you. He was big. And scary."

"Did the ghost see you?" Claire asked Little John. "Did he know you were there?"

"I don't know," Little John said. "I was watching TV, but I heard him in the hallway. He was moaning and groaning, and sort of swaying back and forth. Like this." He raised his arms and teetered from side to side "He was *soooo* big. I was scared, so I hid. I didn't see him during the day. Only at night."

Claire zipped up her suitcase. "Well, I'm not afraid. And neither is Kaz."

"Uhhh . . . ," Kaz said. That wasn't exactly true.

"Are you guys ready?" Claire asked. She held out her water bottle.

Little John backed away. "I think I'll stay here with Beckett and Cosmo tonight," he said.

"Really?" Kaz said. If Little John was so scared of the ghost that he didn't even want to go to the fire station, maybe Kaz shouldn't go, either?

Little John shrugged. "You guys are the detectives. Not me."

That was true. Kaz and Claire were a team. Scared or not, he had to go with her. So he shrank down . . . down . . . down . . . and went into the water bottle.

Claire grabbed her overnight bag, detective bag, and water bottle. Then she and Kaz set off for the fire station.

Brynlee, RJ, and Sparky were waiting at the main entrance when Claire arrived.

"Hi, Claire!" the twins greeted her.

"Woof! Woof!" Sparky got up on his

hind legs and sniffed at Claire's water bottle.

Brynlee laughed. "I don't know why he likes your water bottle so much."

Claire and Kaz grinned at each other. It wasn't the water bottle that Sparky liked. It was what, or rather *who*, was inside the water bottle.

"Hi, Sparky," Kaz said. He wished he'd thought to bring Cosmo. Sparky and Cosmo would probably have a lot of fun together.

"Sparky still won't go into the fire station through the garage," RJ said as he opened the main door to the fire station. Sparky charged through the door.

"He still won't go in the TV room, either," Brynlee added. "So I think the ghost is still here."

There was only one light on in the

back of the office. Nobody worked in the office on a Friday night.

Claire set her bags down on a chair. "Let's see if we can find the ghost," she said as she got out her ghost glass and ghost catcher.

Kaz passed through the bottle and expanded to his usual size.

"Woof! Woof!" Sparky leaped up to lick Kaz, but his tongue passed all the way through him.

"Watch the tongue, Sparky!" Kaz said as Claire and the others moved down the hallway. He swam hard to catch up.

Sparky stayed close to Kaz.

Dick and David were in the TV room. "Hi, kids," they said when Claire, Brynlee, and RJ walked in. Kaz sailed behind them, but Sparky dropped to his belly in the doorway and let out a doggy groan.

"Hi, Dad," Brynlee said. "We're looking for the ghost."

"Good. I hope you find it," Dick said.

The firefighters returned to their TV show. Claire wandered slowly around the room, her ghost glass in one hand and her ghost catcher in the other. Neither she nor Kaz saw any ghosts.

"Can we check the rest of the station?" Claire asked the twins.

"Sure," RJ said.

They checked the kitchen and the sleeping quarters. They peered into the radio room through the window. Sparky trotted along beside them. Everything seemed to be in order. But as soon as they opened the door to the garage, Sparky sat down and began to howl. "Aroooooooooo!"

Claire bit her lip. RJ scratched his head.

"Is the ghost in the garage?" Brynlee asked the dog.

"Ar-ar-arooooooooo!" Sparky howled.

"Let's find out," Claire said as she opened the door. She and the twins went out into the garage and clomped down the stairs. Kaz swam behind them.

Sparky stayed put inside the station.

All the doors in the garage were closed, so Kaz could swim freely. While Claire searched the garage for ghosts, Kaz checked inside the fire trucks and inside some cabinets.

Still no ghosts.

"I don't think the ghost is out here," Brynlee said. "Let's go back inside. Maybe we'll see it during the night!"

"Yeah, I'm hungry," RJ said. "Let's get something to eat."

With Dick's help, the kids baked some frozen pizzas and popped some popcorn. Then they took their snacks into the TV room and watched a movie with the firefighters.

Sparky watched sadly from outside the doorway.

When the movie was over, it was time for bed. Sparky leaped to his feet

and wagged his tail when everyone finally came out of the TV room.

Claire and Brynlee made up beds in one of the bedrooms. RJ rolled out a sleeping bag on the floor in the other bedroom, where his dad and David slept. Sparky pranced back and forth between the two rooms.

"He doesn't know where to sleep!" Brynlee said.

"It's funny he doesn't mind being in the bedrooms," Claire said.

"Why?" Brynlee asked.

"I thought the firefighters said the ghost wakes them up during the night," Claire said. "It steals blankets. If Sparky doesn't like to go into rooms where he's seen the ghost, you'd think he wouldn't want to be in the bedrooms."

"Maybe he never saw the ghost in the bedrooms?" Brynlee said.

"Maybe," Claire said. "That seems kind of strange though, don't you think?"

"I don't know," Brynlee said with a shrug.

But Kaz thought it seemed strange, too.

At 10:30, everyone turned out the lights and tried to sleep. Sparky must've been tired, because he curled up on the floor next to RJ and went to sleep, too.

While the solids slept, Kaz roamed around the fire station, searching for the ghost.

"Hello?" he called out every now and then. "Where are you, ghost?"

The only one who was awake besides Kaz was the person who was working in the radio room. This time it was a man. The screens in front of him were dark, and he was reading a book.

It was a quiet night at the fire station.

Kaz returned to the room where Claire and Brynlee were sleeping. Then he noticed Claire's blanket was gone. Completely gone. *Where did it go?* he wondered.

He glanced over at Brynlee. While he was watching, the blanket that was covering Brynlee started to move. Someone or some*thing* was under her bed . . . pulllling the blanket off her.

Was Kaz about to meet the fire station ghost?

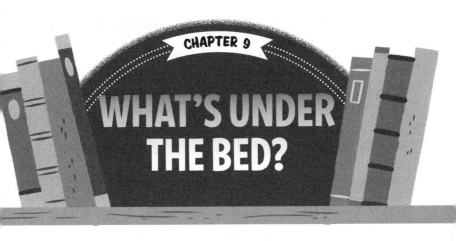

CHAPTER 9

WHAT'S UNDER THE BED?

Kaz hovered above Claire. Watching. Waiting.

"Ohhhhhhhh," a voice moaned. But the voice didn't come from under Brynlee's bed. It came from somewhere else in the fire station.

Kaz peered out into the hallway. He didn't see a ghost.

But he heard it: "Ohhhhhh," it moaned.

Brynlee bolted up in bed. "What's happening?" she asked.

"What?" Claire said groggily. "What's that noise?" She raised her head, then sat up all the way. "Brr. It's cold in here." She shivered.

"I know," Brynlee said, hugging her arms to her sides. She dropped her voice to a whisper. "I think the ghost is here."

"He was under Brynlee's bed," Kaz said. "I saw him pull the blanket off Brynlee. He's in another room now." *Did he take the girls' blankets with him?*

Brynlee reached over and turned on a table lamp.

"My blanket's on the floor," Claire said. She picked it up and wrapped it around her shoulders.

"Oh! So's mine," Brynlee said. But when she tried to pick it up, she couldn't. Someone or some*thing* under her bed pulled back.

Brynlee gasped. "The ghost is under my bed!" she said as she let go of the blanket and scooted to the far corner of her bed.

Kaz frowned. Most ghosts could pick up a solid object like a blanket. But if a solid person pulled on the object like Brynlee did, they would pull it right out of the ghost's hands. Solids were way stronger than ghosts.

"Let's see this ghost," Claire said.

Brynlee backed up even farther and hugged her knees to her chest.

Still holding her blanket around her, Claire got out of bed, dropped to her

knees, and peered under Brynlee's bed.
When she raised her head, she smiled.
Then laughed.

"What?" Brynlee said with a scowl.
"What's so funny?"

"Come look," Claire said.

Brynlee hesitated for a second. She
leaned over just far enough to see under
the bed.

Kaz dove down and took a peek, too.

Sparky was curled up on Brynlee's blanket under the bed.

"Sparky!" Brynlee laughed. "Come out of there. Give me back my blanket!" She tugged on the blanket some more.

Sparky got off the blanket and crawled out from under the bed. He wagged his tail at Kaz.

Kaz tried to pet the dog, but his hand passed through him.

"Now we know who's been stealing blankets during the night," Brynlee said with a pointed look at the dog.

"Yes, but we still don't know why Sparky won't go in the TV room or the garage," Claire said. She paused, then tilted her head toward the door. "And we don't know who's been moaning. Do you hear that?"

"Ohhhhhhhh," the voice moaned again.

Brynlee nodded. She and Claire went to the door and poked their heads around the corner. Kaz hovered above them.

This time they saw a large dark shadow moving across the wall way down the hall.

"That must be the ghost," Brynlee said in a low voice.

"Is there a light switch in the hallway?" Claire whispered.

"Yes. Right here," Brynlee whispered back. She flipped the switch, and the shadow disappeared in the light. But the moaning continued: "Ohhhhhhhhhh."

"Do you need your ghost-hunting stuff?" Brynlee asked Claire.

"I don't know," Claire said. "That doesn't sound like a ghostly moan to me."

It didn't sound very ghostly to Kaz, either.

"Let's follow the sound," Claire said. As they crept down the hallway, the moaning grew louder. And louder. It sounded like it was coming from the kitchen.

Sparky charged ahead into the kitchen as Dick and RJ came into the hallway behind Claire and Brynlee.

"What is all that moaning?" Dick asked, rubbing his neck.

"Did you guys hear it, too?" RJ asked.

"Woof! Woof!" Sparky barked from the kitchen. But it was an excited bark, not an angry or frightened bark.

They all went into the kitchen and found David staggering around, moaning. His eyes were open, but he had a funny look on his face, like he wasn't actually

seeing anything in front of him. Sparky
was right beside him, wagging his tail.

"David?" Dick said, walking over to
him.

"What's the matter with him?" Brynlee
asked.

Dick smiled. "Nothing. He's sleepwalking." Dick grabbed David's arm and gave it a gentle shake.

David blinked and jerked back. "What? What's going on?" he asked. He looked confused. "What am I doing in the kitchen?"

"You were sleepwalking," Dick said.

"I was?" David asked with a yawn.

"And moaning," Brynlee told him. "Really loud."

"I was?" David said again.

"I don't think he was really moaning," Dick said. "He was just talking in his dream. But it sounded like moaning to us."

"What were you dreaming about?" RJ asked.

"I don't know," David said as he yawned and stretched. "I don't remember."

"*You're* the ghost who's been moaning and groaning and banging into things during the night!" Dick said to David. "No wonder you never hear those noises. You're the one making them!"

"So we don't have a ghost at the fire station after all?" David asked.

"I don't know," Claire said. "I don't think so. But we still don't know why Sparky won't go into the garage or the TV room."

If only Sparky could *tell* them what was upsetting him.

Just then the fire alarm sounded. Bright lights came on all over the station.

"Arooooooooooooooo!" Sparky howled.

CHAPTER 10

HELPING SPARKY

F ire!" David said, the alarm blaring all around them. The kids backed against the wall, trying to stay out of the way as Dick and David raced to the garage. They heard the big doors rise and the sirens starting up.

"Come on," RJ shouted over the alarm. "We can watch the trucks from the main door."

Claire, Brynlee, and Kaz followed RJ down the hall. They all crowded around

the glass door and watched as the first fire truck roared out of the garage. Sparky sat behind the kids and howled.

More firefighters raced into the station.

"How did all those firefighters get here so fast?" Claire asked, her hands over her ears.

"Most of them live nearby, like we do," Brynlee said.

In the next few minutes, two more trucks raced out of the garage with lights flashing and sirens blaring. Then the garage doors went down, and all was quiet at the fire station.

Claire rubbed her right ear. "My ears are still ringing," she said.

Kaz's ears were ringing, too.

"Alarms are loud," RJ said. "They have to be to wake the firefighters up during the night."

"Speaking of night," Brynlee said with a yawn. "Should we go back to bed?"

"I'm hungry," RJ said. "I want to get a snack first. Does anyone else want a snack?"

"Sure," Claire said. She looked at Brynlee and RJ. "Hey, you guys have the same pajamas. Is that another twin thing?"

"No," Brynlee said with a scowl. "It's a *mom* thing."

They all trooped down the hall and into the kitchen. Kaz drifted behind them.

Sparky stopped just outside the kitchen door and sat down. "Arooooooooo!" he howled. "Ar-ar-arooooooooo!"

Everyone turned.

"What's the matter, Sparky?" RJ asked.

"Is he afraid to come into the kitchen now?" Claire asked.

"I don't know," Brynlee said. "Come here, Sparky." She patted her legs.

"Sparky, come!" RJ added.

Even Kaz tried to coax the dog into the kitchen. "Come on, Sparky. Follow me." He swam back to Sparky, spun around, and hovered in the doorway to the kitchen. "I'll even let you pass through me. I know you like to pass through ghosts."

Sparky stayed where he was. "Arooooooooo!" he howled. "Ar-ar-arooooooo!"

RJ sighed. "He was just in here ten minutes ago. What happened in ten minutes to make him not want to be in the kitchen anymore?"

"The fire alarm sounded!" Kaz and Claire said at the same time.

"Could that be it?" Brynlee asked

Claire. "Is that why Sparky doesn't want to go into certain rooms in the fire station? Because he heard the fire alarm when he was last in them?"

"He was in the garage when that other alarm went off," Claire pointed out. "Remember? That's when he ran out!"

Kaz thought Sparky had run out because he was chasing the fire truck. But maybe he ran out because he didn't like the alarm.

"Animals' ears are very sensitive," Claire added.

"You know," Brynlee said, tapping her chin. "Now that you mention it, I was here with Sparky another time the fire alarm went off. We were in the TV room that day."

"I bet that's it," RJ said. "The fire

alarm hurt his ears, so he doesn't want to go into any room where he heard the alarm go off."

"What can we do about that?" Brynlee asked. "This is a fire station. Alarms go off here."

"We have lots of books about dogs in the library," Claire said. "Maybe one of them will have some ideas."

"Maybe," Brynlee said.

* * * * * * * * * * * * * * * *

The next morning, Brynlee and RJ walked Claire back to the library so they could look at the dog books.

"Most of what you're looking for is right here," Grandma Karen said as she pointed at a couple of shelves in the nonfiction room.

"Thanks, Grandma," Claire said as

she pulled out a stack of books. She
dropped to her knees, and Brynlee and
RJ plopped down beside her.

Kaz hovered above and watched
as they each chose a book and started
reading.

After a little while, Brynlee said,
"It says here that if your dog is afraid
of loud noises, you're *not* supposed to
comfort him during the noise."

"My book says that, too," RJ said.
"It says that if you comfort your dog,
then that rewards him for showing fear.
It's better to distract him by playing
with him or giving him dinner."

"This book talks about what to do
if your dog is afraid of thunder," Claire
said. "A fire alarm is kind of like
thunder. You don't know when it's
coming."

"What does it say to do?" Brynlee peered over Claire's shoulder.

"It says to record the sound of thunder, then play it back really soft for your dog while you're playing with him," Claire said. "The next time you do it, play it back just a little louder. It might take a while, but eventually your dog should get used to the sound and learn that good things happen when he hears the scary sound. You have to be careful that you don't make the fear worse, though."

"Let's try it," RJ said. "We can record an alarm and play it back."

"Maybe we should talk to the vet, too," Brynlee said. She closed the book in her lap. "Thanks, Claire, for solving our case!"

"I'm happy to help," Claire said.

"Me . . . too . . . ," Kaz wailed.

RJ's jaw dropped.

"Who said that?" Brynlee asked, looking all around.

Claire shot Kaz a quick look, then smiled sweetly at Brynlee. "Said what?" she asked.

"You didn't hear that?" RJ asked. "It sounded like someone said 'me too.'"

Brynlee nodded.

"Must've been another one of those twin things," Claire said with a shrug.

Brynlee and RJ glanced at each other. "Must've been," they said at the same time. Though neither one looked entirely convinced.

Kaz was okay with that. He was just glad they'd solved the case of the ghost at the fire station. And he was glad Little John wasn't really lost. But he sure wished one of these cases would lead to his mom or Pops or Finn.

Maybe next time . . .